THE
SLANT
BOOK

THE SLANT BOOK
By PETER NEWELL
This uphill work is slow, indeed,
But down the slant—ah! note the speed!
TUTTLE PUBLISHING
Boston • Rutland, Vermont • Tokyo

Published by Tuttle Publishing, an imprint of Periplus Editions (HK) Ltd., with editorial offices at 153 Milk Street, Boston, Massachusetts, 02109.

Library of Congress Cataloging-in-Publication No. 67-12304
ISBN: 0-8048-0532-6

Distributed by

North America
Tuttle Publishing
Distribution Center
Airport Industrial Park
364 Innovation Drive
North Clarendon, VT 05759-9436
Tel: (802) 773-8930
Tel: (800) 526-2778
Fax: (802) 773-6993

Japan
Tuttle Publishing
RK Building, 2nd Floor
2-13-10 Shimo-Meguro, Meguro-Ku
Tokyo 153 0064
Tel: (03) 5437-0171
Tel: (03) 5437-0755

Asia Pacific
Berkeley Books Pte Ltd
5 Little Road #08-01
Singapore 536983
Tel: (65) 280-1330
Fax: (65) 280-6290

05 04 03 02 01 00 9 8 7 6 5 4 3 2 1

Printed in China through Palace Press International

PUBLISHER'S FOREWORD

HOW OFTEN have we heard the expression, "They don't make them like that anymore"—of "vintage" automobiles, period houses, Charlie Chaplin movies, etc. Feeling in that way as we do about this book, its reprinting seemed destined as well as a contribution to perpetuating the humor of days gone by; not so much as a means of comparing it with contemporary humor, but merely to recreate something amusing, at a time when all it required was a thing as simple as this book to tickle one's funny bone, rather than today's complex, subtle, sophisticated—and sometimes sordid—brand of what is loosely called entertainment.

The Slant Book, first published in 1910, was one of several written and illustrated by American artist, Peter Newell (1862-1924). His career started as a portrait artist, using of all things, crayons—again showing the contrast of the success achieved in the past without the use of today's great variety of illustrating media. In addition to this humorous piece, Newell also illustrated Lewis Carroll's Alice in Wonderland and Through the Looking Glass and Mark Twain's Innocents Abroad, as well as his own Topsys and Turvys, Peter Newell's Pictures and Rhymes, The Hole Book, and The Rocket Book.

A novelty item, The Slant Book takes one on an adventure of a runaway go-cart (Webster: A baby carriage, esp. one with the front wheels smaller than the rear wheels). The actual slanted pages of the book contribute to the illusion of a hill, down which the cart is accidentally set adrift.

THE
SLANT
BOOK

Where Bobby lives there is a hill—
A hill so steep and high,
'Twould fill the bill for Jack and Jill
Their famous act to try

Once Bobby's Go-cart broke away
And down this hill it kited.
The careless Nurse screamed in dismay
But Bobby was delighted

He clapped his hands, in manner rude,
And laughed in high elation—
While, close behind, the Nurse pursued
In hopeless consternation

An Officer slid off the lid
As Bobby hove in sight,
And bellowed out, "You're scorchin', kid—
I'll run you in all right!"

But down the Go-cart swiftly sped
And smashed that Cop completely,
And as he sailed o'er Bobby's head
Bob snipped a button neatly!

ROCERIES

A funny Son of sunny Greece
Was standing near the curb,
Beside his push-cart, wrapped in peace,
That naught could well disturb

But all at once he got a shock—
The Go-cart speeding down,
Collided with his fancy stock
And littered up the town!

The runaway then swerved a bit
And snapped a Hydrant, short;
Which accident proved quite a hit
Of rather novel sort

The Water spouted in a jet
As much as ten feet high,
And all were soaked and nearly choked
Who chanced to be nearby!

A farmer's wife, Miss' Angy Moore,
Was trudging up the grade.
A basketful of eggs she bore
To barter with in trade

The Go-cart and the Lady met
(Informally, no doubt)
And made a sort of omelette
And spread it round about!

POST
NO BILLS

A Painter on a ladder perched,
Was working at his calling—
Against its foot the Go-cart lurched
And sent the fellow sprawling

His pot of paint came tumbling down
And wrong side up, it settled
About a Chappie's flaxen crown—
Oh, my! but he was nettled!

A German Band across the street
Its way was slowly wending,
Which was a movement indiscreet,
The way that things were tending

The Go-cart struck the bass drum square,
And passed completely through it.
The Drummer madly tore his hair
And said, "Vy did you do it?"

Some Workingmen were putting in
A heavy plate-glass front.
The Go-cart then came rushing in
And did its little stunt

It smashed to bits a crystal pane
Two sweating men were bearing,
And sped on down the slanting plane
And left them mad and swearing!

An Automobile big and brown
Was chugging up the hill,
And met the Go-cart plunging down
With speed that boded ill

At once there rose a noise and din
Of people in dismay.
A Sandwich-man then butted in
And opened up a way!

A Lad was rushing with a Hat
Some Lady had been buying—
The Go-cart caught—and laid him flat,
And sent the hat-box flying

The Hat fell out and settled down
Upon our Bobby's head.
"Say, I'm the swellest kid in town!"
The precious rascal said

ELER

A Newsboy next was somehow hit—
The Go-cart, swift and dextrous,
Contrived to muss him up a bit
And fill the air with extras

One copy Bobby neatly scooped,
And saw this wild display,
In type so bold it fairly whooped:
"A GO-CART BREAKS AWAY!"

THE NEWS
EXTRA!
THE NEWS
EXTRA!

Then as the Go-cart speeded by,
A Bulldog, quite pugnacious,
Seized on the handle on the fly
And clung with grip tenacious

The Go-cart's speed was so increased
The Dog streamed out behind it,
And Bobby turned to pet the beast
Which didn't seem to mind it!

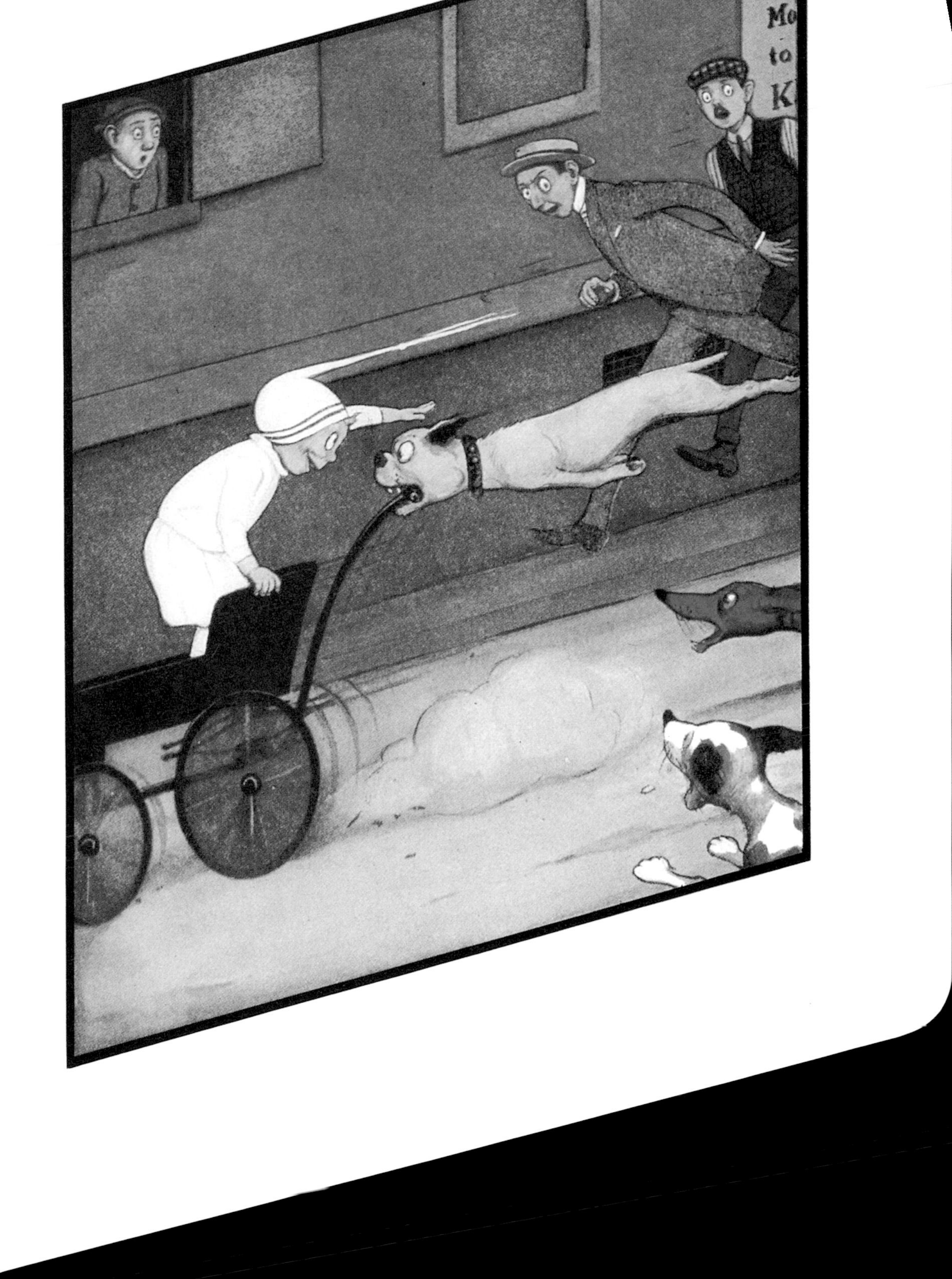

Perambulating down the street
Was Miss Lucile O'Grady—
The Go-cart knocked her off her feet
And took on board the Lady

"Your fare!" said Bobby, with a shout,
One chubby hand extending.
But Miss O'Grady tumbled out
With shrieks the heavens rending

A Herder up the weary grade
A yearling Calf was leading.
The creature was a stubborn jade
And lunged about, unheeding

The Go-cart caught the rope midway
Between the Calf and Herder,
And both fell in behind the shay
With cries of "Ba-a!" and "Murder!"

Two Chappies at a tennis meet
Were battling fast and hard—
The Go-cart skidded off the street
And shot across the yard

The game was "forty all," but then
It didn't end that day—
The Go-cart dashed into the net
And carried it away!

On came the Go-cart down the grade
(The town was now behind it)
And ran into an orchard's shade
Where Providence resigned it!

But then it only grazed a tree
And set it all a-shiver;
The ripened fruit fell merrily
And likewise Sammy Sliver!

Then through a Watermelon patch
This awful cart descended,
And split the melons by the batch—
The Farmer was offended

And tried to stop its wild career,
Which was a silly notion—
It passed him promptly to the rear
With quite a rapid motion!

A Picnic Party on the green
Were seated at their lunch—
The Go-cart dashed upon the scene
And through the happy bunch!

Sardines and pickles, ham and cake,
Were jumbled in a mess.
Then straightway rose these Picnickers
And shouted for redress!

An Artist sketching on the slope
A lively air was humming,
And so absorbed was he, he failed
To note the Go-cart coming

A crash! The circumambient air
Was filled with miscellany,
And damaged quite beyond repair
Was Cremnitz White Mulvaney!

A Damsel milked a brindled Cow
Out in a pasture green,
The Birdies sang from bush and bough—
All Nature was serene

When suddenly a thunderbolt
Dispelled the sweet illusion—
The Go-cart gave the twain a jolt,
And all was wild confusion!

Upon a rustic bridge a Chap
Cast out a bait inviting,
And presently he took a nap
And dreamed the fish were biting

Then came the Go-cart like a gale
And rudely him awakened—
At first he thought he'd caught a whale,
But found he was mistaken!

The longest night must have an end
As well as a beginning;
And so this Cart, you may depend,
Was bound to cease its spinning

It crashed into a hemlock Stump
That chanced to block its way,
And Bobby made a flying jump
And landed in the hay!

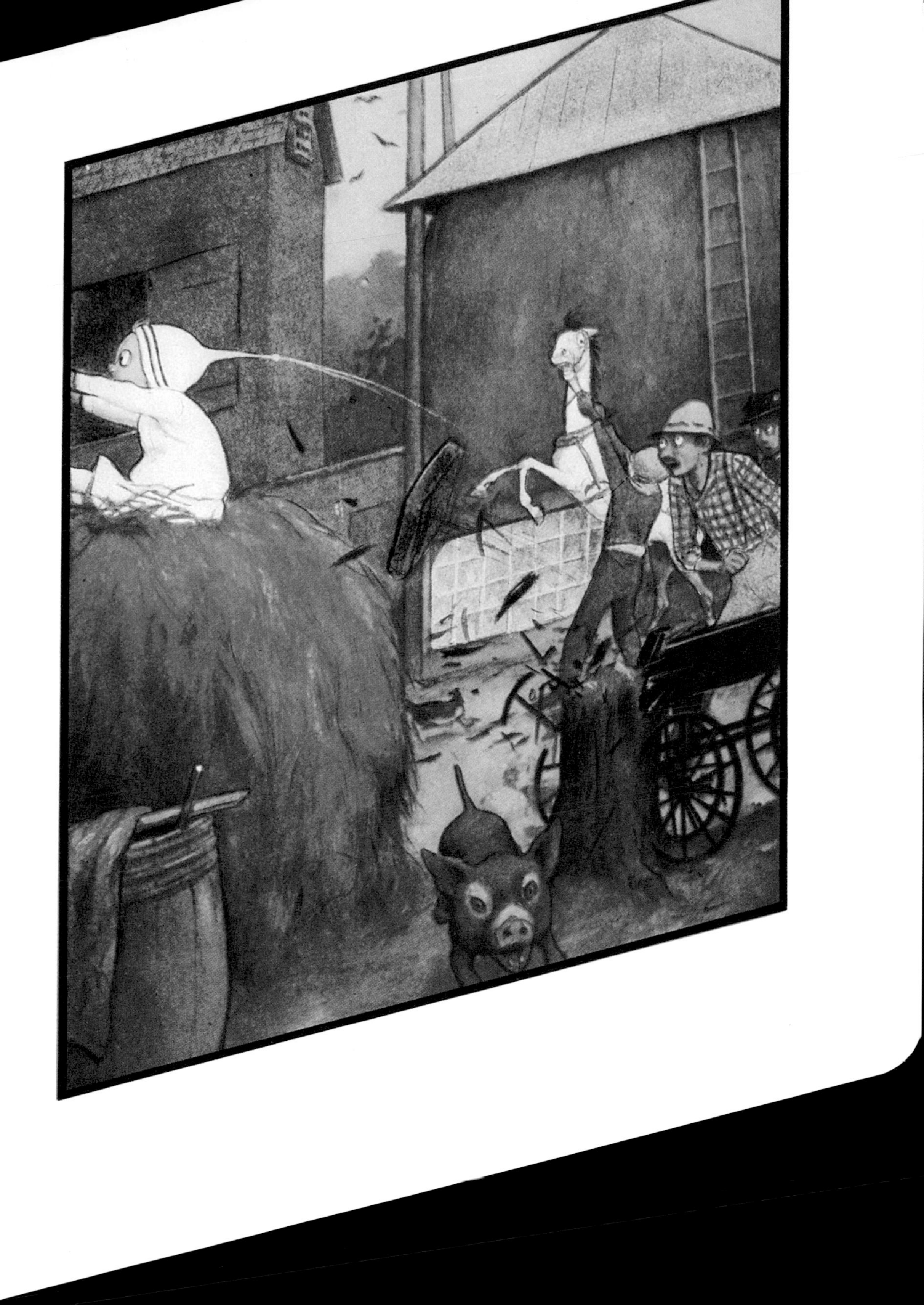